Meg Parker
and the
Lost Dog Mystery

Eleanor Robins

High Noon Books
Novato, California

Cover Design and Illustrations: Herb Heidinger

Glossary: kitchen, minute, paintings, clown, stolen.

International Standard Book Number: 0-87879-440-9

4 3 2 1 0 9 8 7 6 5
4 3 2 1 0 9 8 7 6 5

Write for a free full list of books just like
The Meg Parker Mysteries.

Contents

CHAPTER 1

The Barking Dog

Meg and her mom and dad were in the den.

Meg said, "Dad, I need to go into the city tomorrow afternoon. Is there anything you need?"

"No. Just drive very carefully," her dad answered.

"You bet I will. I think I'll ask Kate to go with me," she said. Kate, her best friend, lived just across the street.

"Sounds like a good idea," her dad said.

Meg hurried to the phone. "Kate, I'm driving my car into the city tomorrow afternoon. Do you want to go with me?"

Kate said, "You know I do. What time do you want to go? And what are we going to do while we're there?"

"Come over here tomorrow morning, and we'll talk about it," Meg answered.

"OK. See you then," Kate said.

Meg went to bed soon after talking to Kate. But she forgot to make sure her cat Muffin was in the house.

A long time later something woke Meg up. It was a dog barking. She turned on the light. Then she looked out her window.

She could see a light on in Kate's room across the street. Kate was looking out her window, too.

Meg could see the barking dog in the light from Kate's window.

Meg could see the barking dog in the light from Kate's window. It was Mrs. Redman's dog. Mrs. Redman lived next door to Kate. Meg couldn't see what the dog was barking at.

All of a sudden, Meg thought of something. She hadn't made sure Muffin was in the house. Now she was worried. Her little sister Amy might have put Muffin outside and forgot to let him back in. Muffin might be what Mrs. Redman's dog was barking at. She had to find out if Muffin was asleep in his box in the kitchen.

Meg turned on the hall light. Then she quietly went down the steps and into the kitchen. She turned on the light. Muffin was in his box.

Meg didn't know her mom was following

her down to the kitchen.

Her mom said, "What are you doing down here, Meg? It's late. You should be asleep. Is something wrong?"

Meg said, "No, Mom. I was just worried about Muffin. Mrs. Redman's dog woke me up. I thought he might be barking at Muffin. I thought Amy might have put Muffin outside and forgot to let him back in."

Her mom said, "You didn't have to worry, Meg. Your dad and I always make sure Muffin is in the house at night."

"I know, Mom. But I just wanted to be sure Muffin was all right. See you in the morning," Meg said.

CHAPTER 2

The Dog Is Missing

Very early the next morning Kate came to see Meg. "When are we going to the city? I can hardly wait to leave," Kate said.

"About 1:00. Will you be ready by then?" Meg asked.

Kate laughed. Then she said, "I'm ready now. What are we going to do in the city?"

"Buy a present for Amy," Meg said.

"What are you going to get her?" Kate asked.

"I'm not sure. We can look around. I know I'll find something she'll like," Meg answered.

"How long will it take us to get there?" Kate asked.

"About 30 minutes," Meg answered.

"I can hardly wait to leave," Kate said again.

Meg said, "Mrs. Redman's dog woke me up last night. I saw you looking out your window at him. Did you see what he was barking at?"

"No, I didn't," Kate answered.

"We haven't been over to see Mrs. Redman in a long time. Let's go see her," Meg said.

Meg told her mom where they were going. Then she and Kate hurried over to Mrs. Redman's house.

Meg rang the bell. Mrs. Redman opened the door. She looked very unhappy.

"Is something wrong, Mrs. Redman?" Meg asked.

"My little dog is gone. I don't know where he could be," Mrs. Redman said.

"Maybe the people next door have seen him," Meg said.

"They aren't at home. They're out of town," Mrs. Redman said.

"Maybe your little dog will be back home in a few minutes," Kate said.

"I don't think so. He's never stayed away this long before. I think he must be lost. Can you two girls help me find him?" Mrs. Redman said.

8

"We can try. We can ride around in my car and look for him," Meg said.

"I know what else we can do," Kate said.

"What?" Meg asked.

Kate said, "We can write a note about him being lost. Then we can put the note on the wall at the Ice Cream Shop. Then other people can help us look for him."

Meg said, "That's a good idea. When was the last time you saw your little dog, Mrs. Redman?"

"When he woke me up barking last night," Mrs. Redman said.

"Do you know what he was barking at, Mrs. Redman?" Kate asked.

"No, I don't. I just wish I'd gone outside right then to get him. I may never see him again," Mrs. Redman said.

"Don't worry, Mrs. Redman. We'll find him," Meg said. She hoped they would, but she wasn't too sure they would. She didn't tell Mrs. Redman that because she didn't want to make her worry more.

"Thank you so much for helping me, girls," Mrs. Redman said.

"We're glad to help. We'll let you know when we find out something," Meg said.

Meg and Kate went back to Meg's house. Meg helped Kate write the note about the lost dog.

"What do you think?" Meg asked as she handed the note to Kate.

"I like it. Let's get it down to the Ice Cream Shop. We can also see Dave and Fred when we're there," Kate said.

Lost

Brown and White Dog

If found, please call 555-7134

CHAPTER 3

The Girls Look for the Dog

The girls went outside and got in Meg's old green car. Meg said, "First we'll ride up and down a few streets near here. Maybe we'll see Mrs. Redman's dog."

"I hope we do. Mrs. Redman looked very unhappy. We need to find her dog right away," Kate said.

The girls rode up and down the streets near Mrs. Redman's house. They looked and looked for the lost dog. But they didn't see him.

"We might as well stop looking. We aren't going to find him. Let's go put the note on the wall of the Ice Cream Shop," Kate said.

"That's a good idea," Meg said.

Meg turned left on Main Street. Then she parked her car in the parking lot next to the Police Station. They got out of the car and locked it.

"Do you have the note, Kate?" Meg asked.

"I sure do. I hope Fred is working this morning," Kate said.

Kate liked Fred a lot.

"I think he and Dave will both be working all day," Meg said. Dave was Meg's boy friend. Both boys worked at the Ice Cream Shop.

Meg and Kate went inside the Ice Cream Shop. Only a few people were in there buying ice cream. They saw Dave, but they didn't see Fred.

"Hi, Meg. Hi, Kate. What kind of ice cream can I get you? Do you want something new today?" Dave asked.

"We didn't come for ice cream this morning. We came to put a note on the wall," Meg said.

A lot of people put notes on one of the walls at the Ice Cream Shop. Many of the notes were about jobs.

"What kind of note is it?" Dave asked.

"A note about a lost dog. Mrs. Redman hasn't seen her little dog this morning. She thinks he ran off and got lost. She asked Kate and me to

14

help her find him. Kate thinks putting a note on the wall here might help."

"That's a good idea. I'll put it on the wall for you," Dave said.

"Thanks, Dave. Will you tell all the people who come in here about the dog? Mrs. Redman is very unhappy about him being lost," Meg said.

"Sure. I'll be glad to," Dave said.

Kate said, "Meg said Fred was working here this morning."

"He is. He's in the back washing dishes. Next time it's my turn to wash them," Dave said.

"Kate, I'm sorry you didn't get to see Fred. It's too bad we can't come back later today," Meg said.

"Why can't you?" Dave asked.

"We're going to the city this afternoon," Meg said.

"That's a good idea. I'll put it on the wall for you," Dave said.

"Why are you going to the city?" Dave asked.

"To get a present for Amy," Meg answered.

"You girls be careful," Dave said.

"We will. We'd better go now. Be sure to tell people about Mrs. Redman's dog," Meg said.

Dave said, "I will. Have you told your uncle Bob about the dog? He might ask his policemen to look for the dog when they're driving around."

"That's a good idea. We'll stop by the Police Station on our way back to my car," Meg said.

CHAPTER 4

The Girls Visit Uncle Bob

Meg and Kate left the Ice Cream Shop. They went next door to the Police Station. They went inside. They walked over to the Police Chief.

"Hello, Uncle Bob," Meg said. The Police Chief was her dad's brother.

"Hello, girls. What can I do for you today? Or did you just come by to say hello?" Meg's uncle said.

"We need your help, Uncle Bob," Meg said.

"What's wrong?" he asked.

Meg said, "Mrs. Redman lives next door to Kate. She's very unhappy. Her dog ran away and hasn't come back. She thinks he's lost."

"We thought maybe the police could help us find him," Kate said.

"I'll ask my policemen to look out for him. That's all we can do. We're staying busy working on a big case right now," Meg's uncle said.

"What kind of case?" Kate asked.

Meg's uncle said, "We're trying to find some men who go around taking paintings from people's homes. But they wait for the people who own them to go out of town. A lot of paintings have been taken lately. But we haven't been able to find out who is doing it."

"I wish we could help you, Uncle Bob," Meg said.

"I wish you could, too. We need all the help we can get. These men are hard to catch," her uncle said.

"Why hasn't someone seen the men taking the paintings?" Kate asked.

"They get into the houses at night. Then the people next door are all asleep," Meg's uncle said.

"Maybe you'll catch them soon," Meg said.

"I hope so. Now tell me what Mrs. Redman's dog looks like," her uncle said.

"He's brown and white and small," Meg said.

Meg's uncle started to write down what Meg told him.

"We rode around in Meg's car and looked for him before we came here. But we didn't see him anywhere," Kate said.

"And we put a note on the wall at the Ice Cream Shop," Meg said.

"You girls have been very busy this morning. Don't worry about the dog. I'm sure someone will find him soon," Meg's uncle said.

CHAPTER 5

A Visit to the City

Meg and Kate left the Police Station. They went back to the parking lot. Meg unlocked her car. They both got in.

They looked for Mrs. Redman's dog on their way back to Meg's house. But they didn't see him.

The girls went over to see Mrs. Redman again.

"Did you find my little dog?" Mrs. Redman asked.

"No, we didn't," Meg said.

Kate said, "But we looked for him. And we put the note on the wall at the Ice Cream Shop. And we told Police Chief Parker that your dog is lost. Chief Parker is Meg's uncle. He said his policemen will look out for your little dog."

"Thank you for all you've done to help me, girls. Maybe someone will find my little dog," Mrs. Redman said. But she still looked very unhappy.

"We'll let you know when we hear anything," Meg said.

The two girls left Mrs. Redman's house.

They hurried and ate their lunch. Then they were ready to go to the city.

The girls got in Meg's car and started on their way. Meg took her time so she would drive very carefully.

Kate said, "This is fun. I wish we could go to the city every week."

"So do I," Meg said.

About 30 minutes later they came to the city. It took Meg a long time to find a parking lot. Then she parked her car. She and Kate got out of the car and locked the doors.

"Where is the store we're going to?" Kate asked.

"A long way from here so we have a long way to walk," Meg said.

Kate said, "That's OK. Walking will do us

good. But don't tell my mom and dad I said that."

Meg laughed.

The girls walked and walked.

They looked at the store windows. They went into a lot of stores. But Meg didn't see anything for Amy.

All of a sudden Meg said, "Wait, Kate. Look!"

CHAPTER 6

The Girls See Something

Kate stopped walking. She said, "Look at what?"

"The painting of a clown in the window of that store. I think my little sister Amy would like it. What do you think?" Meg asked.

"I'm sure she would," Kate answered.

"Let's go in that store. I'm going to buy that painting for Amy," Meg said.

The girls went inside the store. A man hurried over to them. "Can I help you?" he asked.

"I'd like to buy the painting of the clown that's in the window. I really like it. Is it for sale?" Meg asked.

"I think my little sister Amy would like it. What do you think?" Meg asked.

"It sure is. I'll get it for you," the man said. He hurried up to the front window.

A dog started barking in the back of the store.

The man got the painting of the clown out of the window. Then he hurried back to Meg. He said, "Is this the painting you want?"

"Yes, it is," Meg said.

Meg bought the painting of the clown for Amy. Then she and Kate started to look at the other paintings. The paintings didn't cost very much.

The dog in the back of the store kept barking.

Kate said, "I wonder why that dog keeps

barking. I sure wish he would stop. He sounds like Mrs. Redman's dog. I sure hope your uncle Bob has found him by now."

"I hope so, too," Meg said.

The man followed them around the store. He said, "Can I help you with anything else?"

"No thank you. We're just looking," Meg said.

The man looked like he wished they would go. Meg wondered why he looked that way.

"Are you sure there isn't anything you want?" the man asked.

"We're sure. Are these all the paintings you have? Or do you have some more in the back of the store?" Meg asked.

The man's face turned very red. He said, "These are the only paintings we have. We don't have anymore in the back of the store."

Meg didn't think she and Kate should stay in the store any longer. The man acted mad at them. She said, "Let's go, Kate."

Both girls started walking to the front door.

Just as they got to the door a dog ran out of the back room. He jumped up on Kate.

Kate said, "This is Mrs. Redman's dog. What is he doing here?"

CHAPTER 7

The Lost Dog Is Found

The man ran over and picked up the dog. He looked very mad. The dog kept barking and tried to jump down.

"That's our friend Mrs. Redman's dog. What's he doing here?" Kate asked the man.

"I don't know what you're talking about. This is my dog. I don't even know anyone named Mrs. Redman," the man said.

Meg said, "You must have found him this morning. He ran away from home and got lost."

"We'll take him back to Mrs. Redman for you. We live in the same town she does," Kate said.

"Then why all the noise?"
the tall man said.

"I told you this is my dog. I've had him for a long time," the man said.

The dog kept barking, and the man still wouldn't let him down.

A very tall man came from the room in back of the store. He said, "What's going on out here?"

"Nothing," the other man said quickly.

"Then why all the noise?" the tall man said.

Kate said, "That's our friend Mrs. Redman's dog. He got lost this morning. We want to take him back to Mrs. Redman."

The tall man looked very mad. He said, "We've never been to the town your friend Mrs. Redman lives in. This is our dog and not hers."

Meg wondered how the man knew where Mrs. Redman lived. Then she thought of something her uncle Bob had told her and Kate. She looked at Kate and said, "Let's go, Kate. I want to go back to my car. I'm getting tired of holding this painting."

"Not before that man lets us have Mrs. Redman's dog. I know that's her dog," Kate said.

Meg said, "A lot of dogs look alike, Kate. Mrs. Redman may have her dog back now. Let's go. I'm getting tired of holding this painting."

"All right," Kate said. But she wasn't very happy. She didn't want to go without the dog. She was very sure it was Mrs. Redman's dog. She wondered why Meg didn't think it was, too.

The two girls hurried out of the store.

When they got outside, Kate said, "Couldn't you tell that was Mrs. Redman's dog, Meg?"

"Sure I could," Meg answered.

"Then why didn't you say you could," Kate asked.

"Because I thought of something Uncle Bob told us this morning," Meg answered.

"What?" Kate asked.

"He said some men are taking paintings out of people's houses when the people aren't there. The men are doing it at night when the people next door are asleep. The people on the other side of Mrs. Redman are out of town. And they have a lot of paintings," Meg said.

Kate said, "And Mrs. Redman's dog was barking last night. You think he was barking because of those men in the store. You think they were trying to get in the house next door to Mrs. Redman."

Meg said, "Yes, I do. And I think they may have stolen some of the people's paintings. And I think they may have the paintings in the back room of that store."

"What are we going to do?" Kate asked.

"First we're going to lock this painting in my car. Then we're going back to that store," Meg said.

The girls walked as fast as they could to the car. Meg locked the painting inside the car.

"I hope no one takes it before we get back here," Kate said.

"We don't have time to worry about it now. We have to get back to that store," Meg said.

The two girls hurried back to the store as fast as they could. They looked in the front window. They didn't see the two men or Mrs. Redman's little dog.

The girls went inside the store as quietly as they could. They walked very quietly over to the door to the back room. Then they stopped. They could hear the two men talking.

The tall man said, "I told you to get rid of that dog. I told you not to bring it here."

"Don't worry so much," the other man said.

"You should worry, too. Soon those people will come home and call the police. Then those two girls will find out about the paintings being gone. They may tell the police about seeing the dog here," the tall man said.

"So what? The girl with brown hair said a lot of dogs look alike. She didn't think it was the same dog. I'm sure she'll tell the police that," the other man said.

The tall man said, "We can't be too sure of that. Also the police may come here and look around when they find out we sell paintings. We have to get the paintings we stole out of here right away."

In a very low voice, Meg said, "Come on,

Kate. We have to get out of here." Mrs.

Redman's little dog started barking in the back

room.

*In a very low voice, Meg said, "Come on,
Kate. We have to get out of here."*

CHAPTER 8

Uncle Bob Helps

The girls walked quietly to the front door and hurried outside.

"What are we going to do now?" Kate asked.

"Find a pay phone as quickly as we can. I'm going to call Uncle Bob," Meg said.

The girls found a pay phone not very far from the store. Meg called the Police Station in their town. She told the policeman who answered that her uncle Bob was the Police Chief. She told him she was calling from the city. She said she had to talk to her uncle right away.

Her uncle Bob came to the phone right away. He said, "What's wrong, Meg?"

Meg told him about finding Mrs. Redman's dog. She told him about the two men and the paintings. She told him she thought the paintings were stolen from the house next door to Mrs. Redman.

"You and Kate go back to your car and wait for me. I'll be there as soon as I can. I'll call the city police to go on to that store. They can look for the paintings and Mrs. Redman's dog while I'm on my way. You be sure to wait for me at your car," her uncle said.

41

Meg told Kate what her uncle Bob said. They didn't want to wait at Meg's car. They wanted to go back to the store. But they did what Meg's uncle Bob asked them to do.

It seemed like a very long time before they saw him drive in the parking lot. He had Mrs. Redman's little dog with him.

He stopped his car in front of Meg's car. The girls got out of Meg's car and ran over to talk to him.

"Did you find the paintings, Uncle Bob? Were they stolen from the house next to Mrs. Redman?" Meg asked.

"Why did the men take Mrs. Redman's dog?" Kate asked.

Meg's uncle laughed. Then he said, "Not so fast, girls. Give me time to answer. We found the paintings. They were from the house next door to Mrs. Redman. And the men took the dog so he wouldn't wake up anyone in the houses near there."

"Can we take him home to Mrs. Redman now, Uncle Bob?" Meg asked.

Her uncle said, "You sure can. That's why I brought him to you. Just be sure he doesn't get in your way when you're driving."

Meg and Kate got back in Meg's car. They were in a hurry to take the little dog to Mrs. Redman. But Meg took her time so she would drive very carefully.

43

It seemed like a long time before the girls got to Meg's house. Meg parked her car. Then they hurried over to Mrs. Redman's house.

Mrs. Redman was very glad to see her little dog again. She said, "How can I ever thank you, girls?"

Kate said, "We're just glad to see you happy again, Mrs. Redman. That's all the thanks we need."

The little dog started running. The girls turned around to see why he was running. He was after Meg's cat Muffin.

Meg said, "Let's go, Kate. I'll get Muffin. You get Mrs. Redman's dog before he gets lost again."